I STILL... I DON'T... THERE'S NOTHING—

BERGA!

HEY, CLAIRE!

KEITH!

LUCK...

ガシ！

*GASHI
(GRAB)*

ええええ！

WHAAAAAA!

—A!?

グイ！

TUG

!?

YAGU-RUM—

THE PLACES WHERE PEOPLE HAVE WALKED ARE NOT THE ONLY PATHS.

BACCANO!

Original Story *Ryohgo Narita*

Art
Shinta Fujimoto

Character Design
Katsumi Enami

1

Contents

DOTA
(THUD)

...

SO...

WHAT
AM I NOW,
EXACTLY?

1927

NEW YORK

EVER SINCE PROHIBITION STARTED, THE MAFIA HAS BEEN JUMPIN'.

THERE'S A NEW CASINO OVER IN LITTLE ITALY.

HEY, DIDJA HEAR?

YEAH, BUT YOU'RE GOIN' TO A SPEAKEASY TODAY TOO, AIN'TCHA?

DO YOU KNOW WHOSE WALLET YOU JUST TRIED FOR!? HUH!?

DOKA (WHUD)

DAMN BRAT!!

GA

YOU BETTER LEARN TO PICK YOUR TARGETS!

TOO BAD, PUNK.

GA (THWACK)

I DON'T GOT ONE RED CENT TO LOSE TO A STICKY-FINGERED GUTTER RAT LIKE YOU!!

DOKA

...HAD YOU GUYS PEGGED AS EASY MARKS, EVEN FOR HIM.

...HUH. SO THAT KID...

KA (TAK)

YOU LOOK JUST AS DUMB AS I FIGURED.

OH. I SEE.

HUH?

... FACE—

GUY'S GOT A GIRLIE ....

OH YEAH? LOOK WHO'S TALKIN'.

GO (WHUD)

YOU LI'L ...!

BAKI

DOKA (THUD)
GO

DO (WHUD)

!!

BAKI (KRAK)

GA (GRUNCH)

...!

DOZA (SKID)

WHAT WAS THAT ABOUT MY FACE?

HEY... SORRY 'BOUT THAT.

GUI (YANK)

I DIDN'T HEAR YOU TOO GOOD......

DOSHA (THUNK)

BOSO (WHISPER)

COOL...

DAMMIT...

WE'RE A PAIR OF STRAIGHT-UP BAD GUYS.

WELL... I FIGHT, AND YOU STEAL, HUH?

......SAY WHAT?

I'M CAMORRA.*

I'M NOT MAFIA.*

ARE YOU IN THE MAFIA, MISTER?

SASA (GRAIN)
ささっ

*BOTH ARE ITALIAN CRIMINAL ORGANIZATIONS. THE MAFIA IS SAID TO HAVE BEGUN ON THE ISLAND OF SICILY, WHILE THE CAMORRA IS FROM NAPLES.

THE GANDOR FAMILY, HUH...?

THAT'S NOT LIKE THE MAFIA AROUND HERE? THE GANDORS?

BOSU (TMP)
ぽすっ

CAMORRA?

...!

12

DO IT RIGHT NEXT TIME.

IF YOU'RE GONNA PICK POCKETS ON SOMEONE ELSE'S TURF, YOU'D BETTER KNOW WHOSE TURF YOU'RE ON.

MAYBE THEY LOOK ABOUT THE SAME TO YOU...

...BUT THE MAFIA AND THE CAMORRA ARE DIFFERENT.

...THEY RUN THEIR OWN FAMILY NOW ANYWAY.

KA (TAP)

WELL, TO ME, KEITH AND THE OTHER TWO ARE LIKE FAMILY, BUT...

COMPARED TO THEM, I'M...

BOSO (MUTTER)

I WISH THEY'D MAKE ME AN EXEC.

HUH. TOUGH LUCK.

I GOT INTO A TUSSLE WITH A COUPLE OF WEIRDOS.

HM? WHAT HAPPENED TO YOUR FACE?

GON
GON (TUNK)

WELL, IF IT AIN'T FIRO. HERE TO GRAB SOME LUNCH?

HELLO.

KARAN (CLANG)

GA
GACHA (KACHAK)

CHA

IN THAT CASE, HAVE SOME BOOZE AND FORGET ABOUT IT!

ALL RIGHT. TELL THE BOSS I'LL BE BACK TONIGHT.

ZAWA (MURMUR)
ZAWA

......YOU'D THINK THE GUY WAS JUST GOING SHOPPING.

BATAN (PTUNK)

YEAH. IT'S NOTHING BIG.

SORRY, FIRO. OUR KNIFE MATCH WILL HAVE TO WAIT.

GOING TO WORK, RONNY?

FOR REAL!? HE'S WALKING IN ON ANOTHER GROUP BY HIMSELF!?

I HEARD HE'S HEADED TO NEGOTIATE WITH ANOTHER FAMILY.

QUIT SITTING AROUND ADMIRING HIM AND DO SOMETHING MANLY YOURSELVES!

DON (THUNK)

GU (CLENCH)

HE'S CHIAMATORE, A TOP-LEVEL EXEC. I GUESS THAT AIN'T JUST FOR SHOW......

HUH!? ME!?

...YOU HEARD HER, FIRO. CUT BACK ON THE FIGHTING.

YOU BOYS LOOK SET TO STAY TWO-BIT THUGS FOR LIFE.

WHO KNOWS WHEN WE'LL GET A NEW CAMOR-RISTA.

SERIOUSLY UNCOMFORTABLE ASSOCIATES

I'LL GET THE FIRST AID KIT. YOU WAIT RIGHT THERE!!

UH, DON'T WORRY ABOUT IT...

WHAT!? FIGHTING AGAIN!?

FIRO, YOU NARC...!

CHEATING!? YOU SCUM, DID YOU CHEAT!?

S THAT YBACK!?

DAN (BAM)

ダン!!

WAH-HA-HA!!

AWRIGHT!! I WIN!! A STRAIGHT FLUSH!!

I CAN SEE THE CARDS UP YOUR SLEEVE.

RIGHT, PEZZO?

A PICKPOCKET'S NOTHIN' COMPARED TO US.

YEAH, RANDY.

ビクッ (FLINCH)

THAT'S A FORMER PICKPOCKET FOR YA. YOU'VE GOT SHARP EYES, FIRO.

HUH!? W-WELL THEN, I...

I ROBBED A BANK ALL BY MYSELF.

WHAT ARE YOU TWO COMPETING FOR!?

YEARS BACK, I *STOLE A CERTAIN JEWEL* FROM A MUSEUM.

ドキ DOKI

ドキ DOKI (BADMP)

PERFECT TIMING. I HAD A FAVOR TO ASK YOU.

MAIZA!

FIRO.

WORD HAS IT SOMEONE'S BEEN RUNNING A CASINO ON MARTILLO TURF WITHOUT OUR PERMISSION.

!

THERE'S A JOB I'D LIKE YOU TO DO.

A FAVOR?

DO YOU THINK YOU COULD GO LOOK INTO IT?

FEEL FREE TO LOSE YOUR SHIRT.

JUST FIND OUT THE SIZE, THEIR NUMBERS, AND HOW THINGS LOOK INSIDE. THAT'S ENOUGH.

HUH ......? BUT ...!

YESSIR!! I'LL DO MY BEST!!

NO, ERM... IT'S ONLY SCOUTING. YOU DON'T NEED TO DO MUCH...

DON'T DO ANYTHING RECKLESS. PLEASE.

IT REALLY IS ONLY SCOUTING, FIRO.

.........UNDER-STOOD.

I FOLD.

PASHI (SMACK)

HOW'S IT LOOKING?

AAAAH, DAMMIT!!

HAH!

WHO WERE THEY AGAIN? THE MARTILLOS? I DUNNO HOW A PUNY GROUP LIKE THAT SURVIVES IN NYC.

WELL, I GUESS THAT'S WHAT LET US GET IN HERE THOUGH.

PLENTY OF CUS-TOMERS.

NO CONTACT AT ALL FROM THE LOCAL FELLAS.

WHOA...!

EVEN IF IT'S ROTTEN, IT IS THE BIG APPLE. IT'S LOUSY WITH MONEY AND PEOPLE...

WHAT'S UP?

A 35-FOLD PAYOUT!!

ZA (SHUF)

MAYBE I'LL FOLLOW YOUR BET NEXT TIME.

WAY TO GO, KID!

HEY! YOU OVER THERE! BOY!!

WELL, IT WAS A FLUKE, BUT...

WE WERE JUST LOOKING FOR A FEW MORE PEOPLE.

HOW ABOUT SOME POKER?

YOU LOOK LIKE YOU'D SKIN ME ALIVE.

HA HA!

IT LOOKS LIKE FUN, BUT I'M NOT PLAYING WITH YOU FELLAS.

WHA ...!?

POKER, HUH?

YEAH. IT'S BEEN BIG LATELY.

IT'S STILL POKER, BUT DO YOU KNOW THE RULES OF TEXAS HOLD-'EM?

BY ALL MEANS.

CAN I JOIN IN?

22

WE'RE STARTING THE GAME WITH SIX PLAYERS, THEN.

PAKA (POP)

PA

PA (FWIP)

PA

I'VE PLAYED THIS A FEW TIMES WITH SOME OF THE OTHER MARTILLO GUYS.

SU (SHUF)

FOLD.

BARA (SHUF)

KASHA (CLACK)

IN THE FIRST ROUND, YOU BET ON JUST THE TWO CARDS IN YOUR HAND.

CHA (CLICK)

CHA

TON (TMP)

FORTY DOL-LARS.

RAISE.

I FOLD.

TON

BARA

IN THE SECOND ROUND, THREE COMMUNITY CARDS ARE DEALT ON THE TABLE.

...THEN THE FIFTH CARD IS THE RIVER.

IN THE THIRD ROUND, THE TURN CARD GETS DEALT...

TAN (TMP)

YOU BUILD THE STRONGEST POSSIBLE HAND FROM THESE SEVEN CARDS.

QUEEN AND TEN. FULL HOUSE.

TAN

CHIRA (GLANCE)

I'M JEALOUS.

MY, YOU'RE OFF TO A NICE START.

DAMMIT!

ZARARA (CLATTER)

RAISE!

FOLD.

LOOKS LIKE I'M AT THE WRONG TABLE.

SIGH.

AWRIGHT! GOT A STRAIGHT!!

RAISE.

RE-RAISE.

VERY FUNNY.

HA-HA! WHAT'S WRONG, BOY? YOU'RE BLEEDIN' CHIPS!!

THE HOUSE IS KEEPING TABS ON ME SINCE I WON SO BIG AT ROULETTE.

I WONDER HOW MANY OF THESE GUYS ARE IN CAHOOTS WITH THE DEALER...

TCH!

KASHA (CLATTER)

...BUT THEN ANYBODY COULD DO THIS JOB!

MAIZA SAID IT WAS OKAY TO DROP A BUNDLE HERE......

CHA (CLICK)

I GUESS THIS IS WHAT SEPARATES ME FROM THE EXECS...

HA HA HA!

I GUESS YOU'RE STILL A BIT YOUNG FOR CASINOS, KIDDO.

HEH!

HEY, NOW. DON'T GET CRANKY JUST BECAUSE YOU CAN'T WIN.

KASHAN! (CLICK)

GUYS LIKE THESE...

LEMME TELL YOU SOMETHING GOOD, KID.

DO THESE GUYS DESERVE THE MONEY MAIZA GAVE ME?

AND ANYWAY...

IF YOU DON'T BET BIG, YOU CAN'T TURN THE TABLES EVEN IF THINGS GO YOUR WAY!!

THIS IS A GAMBLING HALL.

ALL IN.

PROD HIM A BIT, AND HE LATCHES RIGHT ON.

THAT PIGEON IS SUCH AN EASY READ ...!!

KU (TAP)

?!

I'LL SHOW THE RIVER CARD, THEN.

SORRY, BUT WE'RE CLEANING YOU OUT.

CALL.

FROM WHAT I'VE SEEN, HE'S AN AMATEUR AT POKER. JUST A KID.

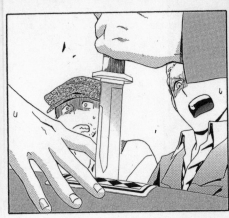

DO
(WHUNK)

HUH?

HOW
DUMB
DO YOU
THINK
I AM?

WHY'D YOU OPEN A NEW DECK AT A WEIRD TIME LIKE THAT?

PAKA (POP)

THE FIRST THING THAT FELT OFF WAS WHEN YOU TOOK A NEW PACK OF CARDS OUT OF THE BOX.

WH... WHAT ARE YOU...?

...IT LOOKED LIKE YOU WERE MIXING 'EM UP, BUT YOU JUST SPREAD THE CARDS OUT WITHOUT CHANGING THE ORDER.

THEN WHEN YOU SHUFFLED ...

TO FIX WHO'LL WIN AND ON WHAT ROUND.

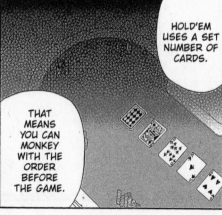

HOLD'EM USES A SET NUMBER OF CARDS.

THAT MEANS YOU CAN MONKEY WITH THE ORDER BEFORE THE GAME.

WHEN THIS GAME'S OVER, I'LL GO HOME.

YOU'RE RIGHT. I'M JUST A SORE LOSER.

YOU JUST SOUND LIKE A SORE LOSER.

BUT...... YOU'VE GOT NO PROOF.

THOSE ARE THE HOUSE RULES... *MISS*.

.... I'LL KEEP THAT IN MIND.

NEXT TIME YOU CALL ME A CHEATER...

...YOU'LL GET YOUR PRETTY FINGERS BROKEN.

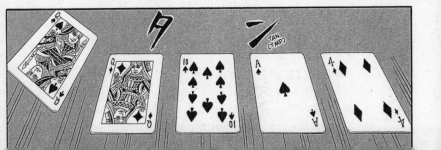

TAN (TMP)

WELL, STUFF HAPPENED, BUT IT LOOKS LIKE THE CHIPS ARE MINE......

QUEENS AND ACES. FULL HOUSE!

Y... YEAH!

A ROYAL... STRAIGHT FLUSH...?

THAT'S NOT HOW I FIXED IT...

THE ODDS ARE 1/650,000... THE ULTIMATE HAND!

NO WAY...... THAT'S NOT POSSIBLE!!

BIKU (FLINCH)

I HATE LOSING.

SORRY.

WHAT DID YOU...?

YOU CHEATED!!?

GA (GRAB)

Y...

34

BOGIN
(SNAP)

GYAAH!!

THAT'S A HOUSE RULE, RIGHT? GOT A PROBLEM WITH IT?

ザワッ
ZAWA
(MURMUR)

!?

TAKE BETTER CARE OF 'EM.

AND AFTER I STOPPED SHORT OF STABBING YOU IN THE HAND...

YOU SWITCHED THEM WHILE WE WERE WATCHING THE KNIFE...?

WAIT, WAS IT THEN...?

WE'LL GET THIS...

APOLOGIES FOR THE COMMOTION, FOLKS!

ZAWA (CLUTTER)

ZAWA

I'M NOT JUST SHARP-EYED. I'VE GOT STICKY FINGERS.

WHA—!?

ZAWA

HEY! THIS DEALER CALLED ME A CHEATER!

WHY, YOU LITTLE...

I GUESS YOU CAN'T TRUST A PLACE JUST BECAUSE IT'S NEW.

I DON'T WANT NO TROUBLE.

I SAID I'D GO HOME AS SOON AS THE GAME WAS OVER, DIDN'T I?

ZA (ZSH)

WHAT?

OH! HEY, YOU! YOU'RE THE...

THAT MARTILLO GUY FROM BEFORE!!

NOW, BEFORE I'M OUTED, I'LL JUST—

I'VE GOT THE LAYOUT OF THIS PLACE DOWN.

CHIRA (GLANCE)

ちら

THEY SENT A SINGLE KID OVER?

HA-HA-HA...!!

HA HA HA! WHAT A CUTE LIL' ASSASSIN!

HUH? THE MARTILLOS?

ARE THE MARTILLOS TRYING TO CRACK US UP OR SOMETHING!?

...THAT'D BE A FEATHER IN MY CAP AS A MARTILLO, WOULDN'T IT?

.... IF I TOOK HALF OF YOU TURF SQUATTERS OUT WITH ME...

HA HA HA!

WHAT
ARE
YOU
TAL—

WELL.
EVEN IF
I DID
THAT...

MINE. AS A
MARTILLO.

NO ONE
ELSE'S.

KA
(TAK)

BUT
EVEN
SO.

...MY BOSS,
MOLSA
MARTILLO,
WOULDN'T
BE HAPPY.

I DON'T
CARE WHO
SAYS YOU
CAN OR
WHAT YOU
PAY...

I WON'T
LET YOU
INSULT
THE MAR-
TILLOS.

...I'LL
NEVER
FORGIVE
YOU.

......?

HUH?

'SCUSE ME. BEG PARDON.

I'M HERE TO TALK TO THE MANAGER OF THIS ESTABLISHMENT.

HUH?

THERE WAS NO ONE AT THE DOOR, SO I LET MYSELF IN.

I DIDN'T TELL YOU TO START A FIGHT, DID I?

FIRO, WOULD YOU GO WAIT OUTSIDE?

HUH ...!? BUT—

I MEAN, HE'S AN EXECUTIVE, BUT HE'S THE CONTAILIOLO ...!!

HIS SPECIALTY'S ACCOUNTING ...!!

...I'VE NEVER HEARD OF MAIZA FIGHTING, EVER! IS HE GONNA BE OKAY!?

...THAT'S WHAT HE SAID, BUT...

IF IT DOES ...

IF ANY-THING HAPPENS ...

...IT'LL BE MY FAULT, WON'T IT......?

GACHA (KACHAK)

LET'S GO, FIRO.

THANKS FOR WAITING.

AH!

PHEW...

I WAS OUT OF LINE...

...I'M SORRY.

I STILL DON'T HAVE...ANY POWER OR SKILLS, AND I...

...I SHOULD HAVE KEPT MY NOSE CLEAN.

LONG OR SHORT, EVERY MAN HAS HIS OWN STRIDE.

GUI
(TUG)

IF YOU RUN FULL TILT TO TRY TO CATCH UP...

...AND MEET WITH AN ACCIDENT, YOU'LL LOSE EVERYTHING.

"MIND YOUR LIFE."

YOU KNOW WHAT THEY SAY—

OH.

......I'M SURPRISED YOU GOT OUT OF THERE WITHOUT A SCRATCH THOUGH, MAIZA.

...... YES, SIR.

...AND THEY LISTENED QUIETLY TO WHAT I HAD TO SAY.

I SHOWED THEM CIVILITY...

WHAT THE HELL WAS......?

ZA
(ZSH)

I DIDN'T COME SPECIFICALLY TO CLEAN UP AFTER HIM, NO.

DID YOU COME ALL THE WAY OUT HERE TO WIPE YOUR ASSOCIATE'S ASS?

THE MARTILLO CONTAI-UOLO?

CHAT, HUH ......?

WE'D BEEN PLANNING TO HAVE SOMEONE COME CHAT WITH YOU.

TODAY JUST TURNED OUT TO BE THE DAY.

BOTATA!
(SPLATTER)

DO
(THUD)

YOU MUST
BE NUTS,
COMING TO
A PLACE
LIKE THIS
ALONE.

AND HEY,
ARE YOU
REALLY A
MOBSTER?

TURNS OUT,
WE DON'T PLAN
TO DISCUSS
ANYTHING.

...I HAVE NO INTENTION OF "DISCUSSING" ANYTHING EITHER.

..........MY APOLOGIES, BUT...

.......HUH?

WHUH?

THE WOUND ......

ズ
ズ (SHLP)
ズ
ズ
ズ
テリ

ズ
(SHLP)
ズ
ズ

I ONLY CAME TO "TALK."

I DIDN'T COME FOR A "DISCUSSION."

MON-STER?

NO.

M......... MONSTER ......!!

THE BLOOD JUST...THE WOUND —!!?

KA (TAK)

WITH A MONSTER, I EXPECT YOU COULD SAVE YOURSELF BY RUNNING TO THE NEAREST CHURCH, BUT........

GA (GYANK)

...EXORCISMS WON'T WORK ON THE MARTILLO FAMILY.

WHEN "PEOPLE" DIE, THEY DON'T COME BACK.

MIND YOUR LIFE.

48

MAIZA.

IT'S A WORLD WHERE THE SPIRAL OF DESTINY...

SO IT IS. WHAT A MESS.

AH.

IT'S TORN.

YOUR COAT SLEEVE.

...BRINGS PEOPLE WHO ARE STILL STRANGERS TOGETHER.

WELL... I'VE WORN THIS SUIT FOR A LONG TIME NOW.

QUIETLY, THE WHEEL BEGINS TO TURN—

NOW LET THE CRAZY RUCKUS BEGIN.

BACCANO!
RYOHGO NARITA✖SHINTA FUJIMOTO
#1: 1927 NY

#2 San Gennaro

CLAIRE!

WHERE'D HE GO?

SHEESH. THAT KID...

DID YOU CALL ME?

ひょこ

HYOI
CYOINO

I TRIED REAL HARD, AND IT WORKED.

HEY, LUCK!

WAUGH!! HOW DID YOU CLIMB ALL THE WAY UP THERE?

IF YOU BELIEVE YOU CAN WHILE YOU DO IT, YOU CAN DO ANYTHING!

THAT'S DAN—

UH— HEY!!

TA (TAP)

SUTA (TMP)

GASH (GRAB)

HONESTLY... YOU GET LESS HUMAN EVERY TIME I SEE YOU......

*PETER PAN WAS FIRST PERFORMED IN ENGLAND IN 1904.

SO YOU'RE SAYING... YOU CAN DO EVERYTHING EXCEPT MAGIC?

PETER PAN?

NO MATTER HOW HARD I TRY, I'LL NEVER BE PETER PAN.*

C'MON, EVEN I CAN'T USE MAGIC.

DAD'S GONNA BAWL US OUT.

WELL, WE FOUND CLAIRE. LET'S HEAD HOME.

GASHI

IF I WORK HARD!

AND YOUR DAD'S A REAL MAFIOSO, SO WHEN HE SAYS IT, IT'S NO JOKE.

GURI (NOOGIE)

GURI

STOP IT, BERGA.

THE BLOOD OATH AT OUR PLACE IS "BE HOME BEFORE DARK."

I MEAN, HE DOESN'T EVEN SHOW US MERCY.

OLD MAN GANDOR'S SCARY WHEN HE'S MAD.

YOU GUYS ARE LIKE FAMILY ANYWAY. THAT MEANS NO SPECIAL TREATMENT.

OF COURSE NOT.

CLAIRE AND I LIVE IN HIS TENEMENT, SO HE'S LOOKING AFTER US NOW TOO.

THE GANDORS' DAD IS AN EXECUTIVE IN A SMALL MAFIA FAMILY.

I'M SURE HE'LL MANAGE TO GET BY ANY-WHERE.

AND YOU SAW WHAT CLAIRE IS LIKE.

I BET THE GANDORS TAKE OVER FROM THEIR DAD.

......
THEN
...

...WHERE DOES THAT LEAVE ME...?

1927, NEW YORK

HEY, SISTER! I GOT AN ORDER!

COMING! JUST A MIN—

GA (GSTUED)

PASHI (SNATCH)

PASHI

KA (TLUNK)

AAH!

YOU BE CAREFUL NOW.

YES, I'M SORRY. THANK YOU VERY MUCH!

YOU OKAY?

WHOOOA!

CLAIRE.

WELL, YOU HAVEN'T CHANGED EITHER, FIRO.

EVEN THOUGH YOU DON'T LOOK ANY DIFFERENT.

YOU'RE AS AWESOME AS EVER, MAN.

I'M GONNA KNOCK YOU DOWN.

DO YOU WANT ME TO SAY YOU'VE GONE FROM "CUTE" TO "SEXY"?

AHEM!

NAH, I'VE CHANGED. DON'T YOU THINK I LOOK MORE MATURE?

YEAH, EXCEPT THE GANDOR BROTHERS WHO "GREW UP RIGHT" ARE MAFIA BOSSES NOW.

...IT'S ALL THANKS TO OLD MAN GANDOR. HE LOOKED OUT FOR US EVEN THOUGH WE WEREN'T FAMILY.

HA HA

WELL, IF WE'VE GROWN UP RIGHT...

LIAR.

NN?

SURE WAS! THE PLACE WAS FULL OF PARTY ANIMALS. I'M A NORMAL GUY, AND THEY RAN ME RAGGED.

HEY, YOU WERE IN THE CIRCUS, RIGHT?

WHOA...! KEITH, LUCK, BERGA!

IT'S BEEN AGES.

...

IT'S BEEN A LONG TIME.

THERE AIN'T NOBODY WHO'S LESS NORMAL THAN YOU, CLAIRE.

DON'T STARE. YOU DON'T WANT TO MESS WITH THOSE GUYS.

YEAH...... THE MAFIA THAT RUNS THIS PLACE... THE GANDOR BROTHERS... RIGHT?

HEY. AREN'T THOSE THREE ...?

URK ...

BY THE WAY, I FIGURED YOU'D JOINED THE GANDORS, FIRO. YOU DIDN'T?

ERGH...

THIS EVEN THOUGH HE SAID, "I'M NOT USING CONNECTIONS TO JOIN. I'M GONNA BECOME A REAL IMPRESSIVE GUY, AND THEN I'LL JOIN THE GANDORS AND BECOME AN EXEC."

HE'S PART OF THAT GANG FROM NAPLES, THE CAMORRA.

NO, HE *DIDN'T*. THE IDIOT.

ガシッ
GASHI
(THUMP)

WE PROMISED NOT TO TALK ABOUT THAT.

WHY DON'T WE JUST PULL 'IM OVER TO THE GANDORS RIGHT NOW?

SO WHAT, IF THERE'S A FIGHT, YOU'RE ALL GONNA KILL EACH OTHER? BUT YOU'RE FAMILY...

BERGA!

...MAYBE. IF I FEEL LIKE IT.

H-HEY, I WAS KIDDING.

QUIT LOOKING SO SCARY, FELLAS...!

I DON'T REALLY GET IT, BUT IS THAT WHAT YOU WANT, FIRO?

A FESTIVAL THEY STARTED IN LITTLE ITALY LAST YEAR.

WHAT'S THAT?

...

IT'S THE FEAST OF SAN GENNA- RO!

N- NEVER MIND THAT! ARE YOU GOIN' TOMOR- ROW?

THEY SAY IN NAPLES, SOMETHING CALLED "THE MIRACLE OF SAN GENNARO" HAPPENS ON THE DAY OF THE FESTIVAL.

IT CELEBRATES NAPLES'S PATRON SAINT, SAN GENNARO.

APPARENTLY, IT WAS BEGUN BY IMMIGRANTS FROM NAPLES TO PASS DOWN ITALIAN CUSTOMS.

THE DRIED BLOOD OF THE SAINT, WHO DIED LONG AGO, BECOMES LIQUID AGAIN.

YOU MEAN THE GUY ALL THOSE CRAZY RUMORS ARE ABOUT?

AH! "THE PHANTOM FATHER," RIGHT?

SPEAKING OF MIRACLES, HAVE YOU SEEN THE TABLOIDS?

HUH!

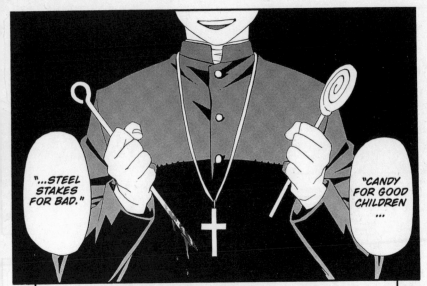

"...STEEL STAKES FOR BAD."

"CANDY FOR GOOD CHILDREN..."

A MURDERER DRESSED LIKE A PRIEST HAD APPEARED IN NYC.

DON'T TAKE IT SERIOUSLY. IT'S JUST A RUMOR.

IF A GUY LIKE THAT EXISTS, I'D LIKE TO MEET 'IM!!

...AND WHEN HE'S CORNERED, HE JUST VANISHES.

I HEARD HE DOESN'T DIE IF YOU STAB HIM...

*SILENT MOVIES WERE MOVIES WITHOUT VOICES OR AUDIO. ACCOMPANISTS PLAYED MUSIC TO GO WITH THE MOVIE.

ガシャーン
GASHAAN
(CRAAASH)

APPARENTLY HE'S TAKEN A SHINE TO A CERTAIN LADY PIANIST.*

KEITH PREFERS SILENT MOVIES* TO FESTIVALS.

YOU DON'T LOOK TOO INTERESTED, KEITH.

...

GATA (CLATTER)

A DRUNKEN BRAWL, HUH?

HUHN!?

WHAT WAS THAT FOR, YA RUBE!?

HUH!?

GUI (YANK)

KA KA (TAP)

YOU STARTED IT—

GUSHA (CRUNCH)

GOSHA (WHUD)

OWWW!!

WHA... WHA ...?

QUIT RAININ' ON OUR PARADE.

GAKH ...

THOSE ARE MY SWORN BROTHERS OVER THERE. WE GREW UP TOGETHER. I FINALLY GET TO SEE 'EM.

BERGA, DON'T MAKE TOO MUCH OF A MESS. IT'S BAD FOR BUSINESS.

PASH! (SMACK)

OR HAVEN'T YOU HAD ENOUGH YET?

ORDINARILY, WE'D GIVE YOU A VIVID, PAINFUL UNDERSTANDING OF *JUST WHO RUNS THIS ESTABLISHMENT,* BUT...

BESIDES, OUR FRIENDS ARE WAITING.

...YOU TWO ARE FORTUNATE.

I-I'M VERY SORRY, SIR! YOUR GATHERING ....

NO, NO.

IT'S FINE. IT'S GOOD TIMING. LET'S GO SOMEPLACE ELSE.

SORRY 'BOUT THE INTERRUP-TION.

KARAN (CLANG)
KARAN

YEEG!

O.......OF COURSE, SIR.

WE EXPECT YOU TO *DO GOOD BUSINESS* TOMORROW.

WHAT HAPPENS TOMORROW?

IT'S PROHIBITION. EVEN PEOPLE WHO DIDN'T DRINK VISIT SPEAKEASIES NOW.

DURING A FESTIVAL, ALL SORTS OF THINGS WILL BE MORE RELAXED.

WE THOUGHT WE'D USE THE FESTIVAL TO EARN A LITTLE EXTRA WITH LIQUOR.

ALTHOUGH UP UNTIL TWO YEARS AGO, THEY STILL CALLED ME "YOUNG MASTER" AND "THE LITTLE GANDOR FIEND"...

YOU'RE MY AGE, BUT YOU'RE LOOKING REALLY GOOD AS A BOSS!

...YOU'RE A SMART GUY, LUCK. JUST LIKE ALWAYS.

WHERE ARE THEY SETTING UP THIS FESTIVAL? SHOW ME!

GASHI (GRAB)

WAUGH!

HEY, LUCK!

ALL RIGHT, JUST STOP DRAGGING ME PLEASE.

BERGA'S USELESS FOR STUFF LIKE THAT.

SAY *WHAT,* CLAIRE!?

ARE YOU OKAY?

AND, UH, GEEZ, KEITH, I HAVEN'T HEARD YOU TALK IN FOREVER!!

...

I...I'M NOT *NOT* OKAY OR ANYTHING.

I DON'T HAVE SOMETHING LIKE THE OTHER GUYS DO, BUT...

SEE...

...

68

......

I DON'T PLAN ON RELYING ON THE GANDORS OR GOD.

...I'M GONNA MAKE IT ON MY OWN, AS FIRO PRO-CHAINEZO.

DA (DASH)

DA

THAT GUY'S A THIEF!! SOME-BODY GRAB 'IM!!

HEY, HOLD IT!!

WAGH!?

DON (WHUD)

OUTTA MY WAY!!

WHOA!

YOU
OKAY?

MAN,
THAT
GUY WAS
FAST...

STOP!
HEY!

HUH...?
OH...!!

EXCUSE
ME. THANK
YOU VERY
MUCH!!

GASA
(RUSTLE)

OH, OF
COURSE
!!

NO HELP
FOR THAT.
HE CAME
UP BEHIND
YOU.

I
COULDN'T
EVEN
REACT...

WOW...
THAT
REALLY
STARTLED
ME.

...UH... THANKS.

A PRIEST AND CANDY... FOR REAL?

HAVE ONE, AS THANKS.

MY NAME IS DONATELLO. I'M A PRIEST.

WOULD YOU CARE TO JOIN US?

IT'S A PUPPET SHOW.

"THEN SAN GENNARO SPOKE."

ALL KIDS.

YES, OF COURSE.

DONATELLO! WOULD YOU COME HELP US CARRY SOME STUFF?

NAH, I'LL PASS.

WHAT A SHAME.

NO OFFENSE.

...

THERE ARE SURE TO BE LOTS OF PEOPLE HERE FOR THE FESTIVAL TOMORROW.

BUTTER MILK HANNES PIZZA

HA HA!

WE'RE QUICKER THAN YOU, FATHER, SO WE'LL BE FINE.

YOU TWO BE CAREFUL AS WELL.

BE SURE TO ENJOY IT TO THE FULLEST.

I BET THERE'LL BE ALL SORTS OF PEOPLE AT THIS YEAR'S FESTIVAL.

WELL, HE'S RIGHT.

THINK THAT PRIEST IS GONNA BE OKAY?

べしゃ
BESHA (SPLAT)

GYAH!

"AND YET, SAN GENNARO RETURNED ALIVE.

"EVEN WHEN PUT IN A FURNACE AND LEFT TO THE MERCY OF THE FLAMES...

"...HE HADN'T SUFFERED A SINGLE BURN."

WHAT'S UP, PEZZO?

NN?

HEY, RANDY. AIN'T THAT LIQUOR?

WAIT! SOMEBODY'S COMIN'!!

THERE, YA SEE!? IT'S WINE!!

WELL, THERE'S A FESTIVAL ON.

SOME OUTFIT'S PROBABLY TRYIN' TA EARN BIG BUCKS.

EVEN A CHURCH WOULDN'T BUY UP THAT MUCH LIQUOR.

AIN'T THAT THE CHURCH'S WINE?

THE STUFF THEY USE IN MASS.

MAN...WE COULDA SNITCHED SOME.

DO Y'KNOW WHERE THE LOCAL COPS'LL BE?

IT MAY BE "FAILED LIQUOR"...

...BUT NO OTHER BOOZE'S WORTH THIS MUCH.

MOVE IT CAREFULLY.

CARRY IT OUT AND DON'T LOSE A SINGLE BOTTLE.

THE NEIGHBOR-HOOD'S GOTTEN QUITE LIVELY, HASN'T IT?

MAIZA!

YOU DO, HUH?

SADLY, I HAVE TO WORK.

FIRO.

AREN'T YOU GOING TO THE FESTIVAL TODAY?

YOU BE CAREFUL TOO, MAIZA.

I'LL BE FINE. I'M NOT A KID.

IT'S FINE TO ENJOY THE FESTIVAL...

...BUT DON'T GET TOO CARELESS.

I GUESS I'LL STOP BY ALVEARE.

HUH?

PICHON (SPLISH)

IF I TAKE THE ALLEYS, IT'S PRETTY CLOSE—

...THE THIEF FROM YESTER-DAY...?

....! THAT'S ...

AH, MY SAN GENNARO, PRAY TELL ME...!!

PEOPLE WHO'VE LIVED EARNESTLY, FAITHFULLY... WHY!!?

KA (TAK)

WHY MUST THOSE WITHOUT SIN SUFFER FOR THE SAKE OF EVIL...!?

THEY'RE EVERY-WHERE.

...NEW YORK IS AN INCRED-IBLE PLACE.

VILLAINS AND SCUM.

YOU CAN KILL THEM AND KILL THEM, BUT THERE ARE ALWAYS MORE.

THEY BREED LIKE MAGGOTS...

...AND SWARM LIKE ANTS...!!

YES, THE MAFIA ...!!

THE MAFIA ...

バキ

BAKI (CRACK)

THEY INFEST NEW YORK

#3 Determination

SO THE BOSS DIED?

...AND PRACTICALLY SHOVED IT OFF ONTO MR. GANDOR IN THE FIRST PLACE.

THE LAST GUY COULDN'T HANDLE THE TERRITORY...

THIS OUTFIT'S DONE FOR.

IN THAT CASE, WHY NOT JUST SELL IT OFF TO SOME OTHER ORGANIZATION?

AS A MATTER OF FACT, I'M TALKING WITH ANOTHER OUTFIT ABOUT......

NO NEED FOR THAT.

MAYBE WE SHOULD SET UP A SUBSTITUTE BOSS...

EVEN IF THEY'RE HIS SONS, WE CAN'T PULL KEITH AND HIS BROTHERS INTO THIS.

TO THE VERY END, OUR DAD TRIED TO PROTECT THIS TERRITORY.

BERGA! LUCK...!

...TO INHERIT HIS PRIDE.

THAT BEING THE CASE, IT'S OUR JOB...

KEITH...

カ KA

カ KA

カ KA

カ KA (TAK)

カ KA (TAK)

#3 Determination

THE THREE OF US WILL TAKE OVER THE GANDOR FAMILY.

......YEAH. WHAT ABOUT THERE?

...I SEE. ALL RIGHT.

KACHA (CLATTER)

THEY HAVEN'T SEEN MR. KEITH AT THE GAMBLING DEN OR THE BOOKIE'S.

GAN (BAN)

DAMMIT!! WHAT THE HELL IS THIS......!!?

...WE WEREN'T HAVING ANY TROUBLE WITH THE NEIGHBORING OUTFITS.

WHAT'S GOIN' ON!?

YOU CAN'T, BERGA....!

DAMMIT!! I'M GONNA GO CHECK AROUND AGAIN!!

IS THIS SOME KIND OF JOKE, KEITH......?

IF WE PANIC AND THE OTHER OUTFITS CATCH ON, THINGS COULD GET UGLY.

WE DON'T KNOW WHO DID IT, OR WHY, OR ANYTHING.

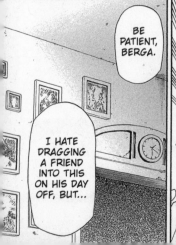

BE PATIENT, BERGA.

I HATE DRAGGING A FRIEND INTO THIS ON HIS DAY OFF, BUT...

WE CAN'T JUST SIT HERE, LUCK! NOT *NOW*......!

YES, SIR.

NICOLA, YOU LOOK OTHER PLACES AS WELL. DON'T LET YOUR MEN CATCH ON.

...I'LL ASK CLAIRE TO SEARCH IN A **PROFESSIONAL** CAPACITY.

LOOKS LIKE THINGS MAY GET A BIT ROUGH.

HM.

I DOUBT THE MARTILLOS WILL GET PULLED INTO THIS, BUT IT WON'T HURT TO BE CAREFUL.

... WELL, NEVER MIND.

IN THIS WORLD, YOU NEVER KNOW WHAT MIGHT HAPPEN.

IS IT A WARNING FROM SOME OTHER OUTFIT OR SOMETHING?

WHAT THE...?

AH!

カ
KA (TAK)

カ
KA

...AH, DAMMIT!

I'D BETTER GET TO ALVEARE AND REPORT THIS.

WELL, I DON'T WANT TO GET INVOLVED IN POLICE BUSINESS.

...I'VE GOT A REAL BAD FEELING ABOUT THIS...!!

EVEN THOUGH THERE'S A FESTIVAL ON...

IT SOUNDS LIKE A GANDOR BOSS GOT HIMSELF KIDNAPPED BY SOMEBODY.

UM...

FIRO, HM?

?

GOOD TIMING. YOU LISTEN TO THIS TOO.

I HAVEN'T HEARD THAT THEY'VE BEEN FIGHTING WITH ANYONE, AND WE DON'T KNOW WHO DID IT.

ZAWA (MUTTER)

WE DON'T HAVE ANY DETAILS.

JUST GOING STRAIGHT FOR THE BOSS. WHAT INSOLENCE.

NO WARNING.

NO ROOM FOR NEGOTIATIONS.

SINCE WE DON'T, WE NEED TO BE CAREFUL TOO.

ONE WRONG STEP, AND YOU PLUNGE ALL THE WAY TO THE BOTTOM, HEADFIRST.

BUT THAT'S LIFE IN THE UNDERWORLD.

THE MARTILLO FAMILY IS SMALL, BUT IT'S STILL AN INDEPENDENT OUTFIT.

NEW YORK'S CROWDED WITH MAFIA.

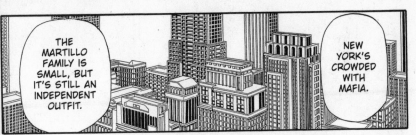

IN FACT, THE GANDORS' SITUATION IS SIMILAR, AND THEY GOT HIT.

...AT A GLANCE, SOME MIGHT THINK WE'RE AN EASY MARK.

WE'RE PROUD OF NOT HAVING CONTRACTED WITH ANY OF THE BIG GUYS, BUT...

GOT IT?

STAY ON YOUR GUARD SO YOU DON'T GET PULLED INTO ANY TROUBLE.

I KNOW THIS IS PUSHING IT, BUT...

YAGU-RUMA!

DON'T TALK NON-SENSE ......

...WOULD YOU...GIVE ME PERMISSION TO HELP THE GANDORS?

GASH (GRAB)

PLEASE ...!

GUWA (FLIP)

BITA (HALT)

...BUT THAT WOULDN'T END IT NOW.

IF YOU WERE JUST A THIEVING BRAT, I COULD THROW YOU, AND THAT'D BE THE END OF IT...

YOU'RE ONE OF OUR GUYS NOW.

...I DON'T PLAN TO HELP THE GANDOR ORGANIZATION.

PLEASE LET ME MAKE SURE MY BROTHER'S SAFE, AS FIRO PROCHAINEZO!!

KA (TAK)

BUT I GREW UP WITH THE GANDOR BROTHERS... THEY'RE LIKE FAMILY TO ME...!

I'LL REGRET IT SO MUCH IT'LL KILL ME!!

IF I DON'T GO NOW, I'LL ALWAYS...

WOULD YOU RATHER JUST DIE HERE, THEN?

HYU (SWISH)

DOKUN (BADMP)

!!

DAN (WHOK)

SHA (SHING)

IF YOU TURN IT ON ME WHEN I COME BACK...

I'M... LEAVING MY KNIFE HERE.

...I'LL TAKE EVERY-THING YOU DISH OUT.

YOU BLASTED IDIOT.

...YOU'VE BEEN WARNED.

BUT I CAN'T DIE YET!

...THANK YOU VERY MUCH...

KA
(TAK)

FOR NOW, I NEED TO FIND OUT ABOUT THE GANDORS...

THERE YOU ARE! HEY, FIRO!!

KEITH?

YOU HAVEN'T SEEN KEITH TODAY, HAVE YOU?

I'VE BEEN LOOK-ING FOR YOU!

CLAIRE!

HE SAID THEY FOUND KEITH'S BLOODY JACKET AND A SMASHED LOLLIPOP IN A NEARBY ALLEY.

LUCK CALLED ME UP.

...LIKE THIS?

YOU MEAN...

CANDY ......?

A PRIEST, HUH......? FINDING HIM IN THIS FESTIVAL WILL BE A JOB AND A HALF.

I WAS WITH KEITH AT THE TIME...

A PRIEST NAMED DONATELLO GAVE IT TO ME YESTERDAY. JUST TO ME......

WHAT ARE YOU TALK—

BA (LEAP)

HUH?

WELL, I'LL LOOK FOR HIM *FROM UP TOP.*

DON'T PUSH YOURSELF, FIRO!

WHOA...

TA (TMP)

TA

TA

YOU'VE GOT YOUR OWN POSITION TO WORRY ABOUT!

I KNOW THAT.

I ALSO KNOW I CAN'T DO ANYTHING SPECIAL... NOT LIKE YOU.

TCH! IT'S BLOCKED OFF FOR THE FESTIVAL?

EVEN SO, I'LL DO WHAT I CAN...

IF I DON'T, THERE WAS NO POINT IN RISKING MY LIFE!!

97

SORRY, NO. WE HAVEN'T SEEN ANY PRIESTS.

HUH?

DID YOU SEE A PRIEST WHILE YOU WERE DRIVING AROUND HERE?

HEY, GOT A SECOND?

KON

KON (TAP)

WHO WAS THAT KID?

I SEE. THANKS.

!! A PRIEST ...!?

HE SAID HE WAS LOOKING FOR A PRIEST.

THAT'S RIGHT. AND *YOUR* JOB IS TO TRANSPORT THIS LIQUOR.

...IT'S NOT OUR PROBLEM.

THAT'S THE GUY'S JOB.

YEAH. BUT EVEN IF HE'S LOOKING FOR *THE ONE WE KNOW*...

THIS "LIQUOR" IS AS VALUABLE AS *THAT MIRACLE*.

THE HOLY SAN GENNARO RETURNED UNHARMED FROM A BLAZING FURNACE...

WAAAH...

COULD HE REALLY BE...?

COME TO THINK OF IT, THE PRIEST WAS THERE WHEN I SAW THAT THIEF TOO.

I'M SEEING MORE COPS...

DID THEY FIND THE BODY I SAW?

"STEEL STAKES FOR BAD."

"CANDY FOR GOOD CHILDREN."

THE FESTIVAL'S IMPORTANT TO THE PRIEST TOO...... IS THAT WHY?

IS HE KEEPING HIS ACTIVITY AWAY FROM THE FESTIVAL ON PURPOSE?

THINK! THAT CORPSE WAS QUITE A WAYS FROM LITTLE ITALY.

WHO GAVE YOU THAT CANDY?

HEY, GOT A MINUTE?

100

A MAFIA FIGHT, HUH? MAN, I WISH THEY'D GIVE US A BREAK...

DIDJA HEAR? THERE WAS SOME KINDA MURDER.

......THERE ARE SO MANY GOOD CHILDREN IN THIS CITY. I JUST CAN'T RESIST GIVING THEM THINGS.

ARE YOU HANDING OUT CANDY TO POOR KIDS ALL THE WAY OVER HERE?

THE OTHER PRIESTS ALL LOOK PRETTY BUSY.

...BUT I'M NOT A GOOD GUY.

YOU GAVE ME CANDY YESTERDAY...

YOU HAD THE WRONG IDEA HERE.

BAKIN CCRACKO

I'M FIRO PROCHAINEZO. A MARTILLO ASSOCIATE.

EVEN WITH MY DYING BREATH, THAT AIN'T GONNA CHANGE.

I'M CAMORRA.

OH...

THERE WAS A GUY WITH ME YESTERDAY... KEITH. WHAT DID YOU DO WITH HIM?

YOU WERE A GOOD BOY, BUT YOU'RE MAFIA...?

OH...! THIS CITY IS SINFUL INDEED...

THEN THERE'S NO HELP FOR IT.

I'LL GIVE *THAT* TO YOU EQUALLY.

NEVER FEAR. GOD IS IMPARTIAL.

...I'LL GIVE YOU THREE CANDIES.

TO (TMP)

IF YOU DO THREE GOOD DEEDS...

IF YOU DO THREE BAD DEEDS...

SHU (SLIDE)

KA (FLASH)

...I'LL GIVE YOU THREE STAKES.

#4 Devotion

...I'LL HIT YOU WITH A PILE DRIVER.

IN THAT CASE...

MISHI (CREAK)

#4 Devotion

!?

AAAH!

BOKI (SNAP)

DOKA (THWOK)

SEE, YOU TRIED TO MESS WITH MY FAMILY.

I DON'T FEEL GREAT ABOUT HITTING A PRIEST, BUT THERE'S NO HELP FOR IT.

BESIDES, LUCK ASKED ME TO DO THIS ONE AS A "JOB"......

ズ ZU (SHLP)

ズ ZU

AS LONG AS HE'S ALIVE, WE CAN GET KEITH'S LOCATION OUT OF HIM ANYTIME WE WANT, RIGHT?

THE GUY'S OUT COLD.

CLAIRE... THANKS FOR SAVING ME, BUT...

...TRY TO DIAL IT BACK A BIT.

ゆら YURA (TOTTER)

!?

NO... SOMETHING'S OFF.

HUH...... HE'S TOUGHER THAN I THOUGHT.

WHY... DOESN'T HE HAVE A SCRATCH ON HIM!?

I AM UNDER DIVINE PROTECTION.

JUST LIKE SAN GENNARO, WHO WAS BURNED IN A GREAT FURNACE, YET EMERGED UNHARMED...

...THE RIGHTEOUS WILL REVIVE AGAIN AND AGAIN.

...I CONTINUE TO WREAK JUDGMENT ON CRIMES THAT HAVE GONE UNPUNISHED.

THAT'S WHY...

DO (SHUNK)

KA! (TAK)

NEW YORK IS FULL...

...OF UNDISCIPLINED SCUM.

ズイ
ZUI (CLOOM)

ググ
(GUGU (TUG)

!

ガ
GA (WHUD)

ガ
GA

YOU'VE GOT GOOD MOVES FOR A PRIEST!

OOPS.

ゴ
GO (THOOM)

...SOMETHING'S REALLY WRONG WITH THIS GUY...

バキ
BAKI (CRACK)

...SO ARE YOU...THE "PHANTOM FATHER"?

HIS WOUNDS HEAL UP...!

WOULD YOU GET REAL!!?

OH, I SEE! IT'S A MAGIC TRICK, HUH!?

NEW YORK IS DEPRAVED, BUT AFTER THIS FESTIVAL OF SAN GENNARO, IT WILL BE REBORN.

IT'S ALL PART OF GOD'S PLAN.

YOU MEAN THE GANDOR BOSS...? KEITH?

FIRST, AT THE END OF THE FESTIVAL, THE MAFIA WILL BE GIVEN A WARNING... YOU SEE?

WHAT WAS IT YOU SAID...? THE MARTILLOS?

ALTHOUGH I COULD HAVE CHOSEN ANOTHER MAFIA FAMILY...

I'VE BEEN ADVISED TO BEGIN WITH OUTFITS THAT CAN BE EASILY CRUSHED, TO AVOID PULLING DECENT PEOPLE INTO THE CONFLICT.

I'M BEING KIND, IN MY OWN WAY.

ALL SCUM LOOK THE SAME TO ME.

BEG PARDON.

...THE MARTILLOS AREN'T MAFIA.

WE'RE CAMORRA.

...BUT IT'S NOT LIKE HE'S THAT FAR OFF BASE, YOU KNOW?

HE DISSED YOUR FAMILY, AND I GET THAT YOU'RE MAD...

HANG ON, FIRO.

WHY, YOU...

ダラ
(DA)
(DASH)

IN THAT CASE, LET ME REAWAKEN YOUR SENSE OF GUILT......

I MEAN, WE *ARE* WITH THE MOB!

DO
(WHUD)

RRGH!

GA
(KICK)

GOKI
(KRIK)

DOGO
(CRASH)

TAN

TA
(TMP)

TON
(TAP)

OH, COME ON...

GA
(WHUD)

GOKI
(SNAP)

DOKA
(THUD)

THIS IS THE PROBLEM WITH SUPER-MEN...!!

GO
(WHAM)

HE LEAVES NO ROOM TO STRIKE BACK.

HE DOESN'T HESITATE TO HURT PEOPLE...!!

WHAT ON EARTH...

...IS THIS MAN!?

WHAT ...ARE YOU!?

GOHO
(COUGH)

YOU...

HUH...?

WELL, I'M *JUST A HIT MAN.* DON'T WORRY ABOUT IT.

IT'S HARD TO SUM ME UP IN A WORD, BUT...

BAKI
(CRACK)

ZA
(RUSH)

CLAIRE!

BA
(LUNGE)

HEY!

!

IF HE RAN, I FIGURED HE'D TRY TO BLEND IN WITH THE FESTIVAL CROWD, BUT...

LITTLE ITALY'S THE OTHER WAY...!

FIRO, DON'T!!

ア！ TAN (T.MP)

I NEED TO REGROUP...

DO (WHUMP)

BEKI
(SNAP)

BAKI
(CRACK)

DOKA
WHUMP

DO
(SHUNK)

SUTA
(TMP)

FIRO,
YOU
OKAY?

HUH!?
WHAT'S
THAT,
SARCASM?

YOU
REALLY
ARE A
GENIUS!

HEY,
YOU'RE
ALIVE!

...DON'T
JUST COME
DOWN
HERE LIKE
IT'S EASY,
JERK.

AND ANYWAY, ISN'T IT POINTLESS SINCE I JUST GOT HIM KILLED?

SEE!? SARCASM!!

NAH, I COULDA DONE IT, BUT A NORMAL GUY WOULD'VE DIED!

NO...... EVEN SO, YOU'RE A GENIUS.

EVEN WHEN IT LOOKS NUTS, HE ALWAYS SURVIVES WITH MINIMAL DAMAGE.

OWW...

SOMETIMES FIRO JUST MOVES, WITH NO HESITATION.

HUH?

HEY, CLAIRE...

ALTHOUGH......

I BET THE OTHER GU HAVEN'T NOTICED MAYBE N EVEN HIM

THAT GUY WAS DEAD... WASN'T HE?

YEAH, SORRY.

HAVE THEY I.D.'D THE GUY WHO WAS STRUNG UP?

ASSISTANT INSPECTOR EDWARD! THE CRIME SCENE IS THIS WAY.

I HAVEN'T SEEN THAT OFFICER AROUND HERE BEFORE...

......HAVING AN INFORMANT ON THE POLICE FORCE SURE MAKES IT EASIER TO MOVE.

BARNES! CHECK THE LIQUOR!

I KNOW. YOU DON'T HAVE TO TELL ME.

SQUEAK!

TCH! SURLY OLD GUY.

THIS IS A NEW DISTILLERY SOME MUCKETY-MUCK SET UP FOR US, YOU KNOW?

GUSHA (SPLLLTCH)

SQUEAL!

ZU ZU (SHLP)

...AND *THIS* IS THE "FAILED" STUFF?

ZU ZU ZU ZU

STILL... THAT'S A MIRACLE TO RIVAL SAN GENNARO'S.

NOT FAILED LIQUOR THAT MERELY PREVENTS PHYSICAL DEATH.

WHAT THE MASTER WANTS IS A "COMPLETE PRODUCT."

SQUEAK

SQUEAK

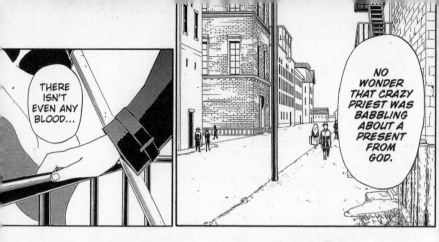

THERE ISN'T EVEN ANY BLOOD...

NO WONDER THAT CRAZY PRIEST WAS BABBLING ABOUT A PRESENT FROM GOD.

HE'S QUIET, BUT WHAT HE DOES IS BIGGER AND LOUDER THAN ANYBODY ELSE.

HE WON'T JUST SIT THERE.

DAMMIT...! NOW WE WON'T GET KEITH'S LOCATION...

CALM DOWN, FIRO! IT'S KEITH, REMEMBER?

NOPE.

...ARE YOU SAYING I WOULDN'T BE ANY HELP?

LEAVE KEITH TO ME.

スタ...
SUTA (TMP)

BESIDES, THANKS TO YOU, WE KNOW ROUGHLY WHERE THAT GUY'S HEADED.

...MISTER CAMORRA ASSOCIATE.

TON (TMP)

I'M WORRIED ABOUT YOU TOO...

WE'RE NOT THAT WEAK.

YOU DID WHAT YOU NEEDED TO DO.

JUST TRUST YOUR FAMILY FOR THE REST.

THE REST IS ALL YOURS.

...... RIGHT.

124

AFTER ALL, SAN GENNARO'S PROTECTION HASN'T LEFT ME......

I'M NOT THROUGH YET. I HAVEN'T LOST TO "EVIL."

DAM-MIT... DAM-MIT...!

WHAT AN AWFUL THING TO......

YORO (STAGGER)

MY CHURCH ....

!?

GOOO! (FOOOOOM)

FROM THE FLAMES... UNHARMED...

IT CAN'T BE... THAT'S JUST...BUT THEN...

HE MIGHT AS WELL BE SAN GENNARO......

IT DID MAKE IT EASY TO FIND YOU THOUGH.

AND GEEZ, MAN, YOU PULLED OUT ALL THE STOPS AGAIN!

KEITH! YOU'RE OKAY?

NEXT TIME I SEE HIM, I'LL KILL HIM FOR SURE.

SORRY ABOUT THAT. LUCK HIRED ME FOR THIS, BUT I LET THE GUY WHO GRABBED YOU GET AWAY.

I'LL END HIM SO GOOD, I'LL LEAVE A POOL OF BLOOD...

GATA
(CLATTER)

KEITH
...!

THAT'S INSANE! BOSSES SHOULDN'T DO THINGS LIKE THAT!!

!? SO WHAT, YOU GOT CAUGHT ON PURPOSE!?

...NO OTHER OUTFITS WERE IN ON IT.

SUTA
(STRIDE)

スタ
スタ
SUTA

YEESH... THAT WAS BAD ON THE HEART.

YOU'RE ALL RIGHT! THANK HEAVENS...

WE STILL HAD TWO.

YOU'D BETTER THANK FIRO TOO.

THAT ISN'T WHAT I... FOR THE LOVE OF... ARGH...!

HE'S FINE.

SAY WHAT!? FIRO DID? IS *HE* OKAY!?

IF FIRO HADN'T FOUND THE PRIEST FIRST AND KEPT HIM BUSY, KEITH WOULD'VE HAD A TOUGHER TIME MOVING ON HIS OWN.

NI (GRIN)

FIRO'S A POPULAR GUY.

FIRO!? WHAT HAPPENED TO YOUR FACE!?

BIKU (FLINCH)
ビクッ

I GUESS I PROBABLY... LOST THE RIGHT TO JUST GO BACK TO THE MARTILLOS AS USUAL ......

MAYBE IT WAS FOR MY FAMILY, BUT I IGNORED YAGURUMA'S WARNING.

WHAT DID YOU DO THIS TIME?

AAH... COME ON! HURRY AND GET THAT TREATED!!

HUH?

WAIT.

MAIZA...

MAIZA.

I'LL BE RIGHT BACK!

!?

BACHIN (SMACK)

!!

IT'S FIRO PRO-CHAINEZO. I JUST GOT BACK.

THAT'S RIGHT...... I HAVE TO GO FACE THE MUSIC FOR THIS...

DIDN'T I DECIDE TO TAKE WHATEVER THEY DISHED OUT...!?

WELCOME BACK, FIRO.

...AND? WAS *YOUR FAMILY* ALL RIGHT?

MOLSA MARTILLO
MARTILLO FAMILY
CAPOSOCIETÀ

BOSS ...!

I HAVE NO REGRETS.

......I DID WHAT I COULD, SIR.

...!

AH, I GUESS WE SHOULD TREAT THAT WOUND FIRST, HM?

LIA! BRING FIRO SOME FOOD.

I SEE.

AND SO NOW...I'LL USE MY LIFE ONLY FOR MY OTHER FAMILY, THE MARTILLOS.

THEN IT'S FINE.

YOU WENT TO HELP YOUR FAMILY, DIDN'T YOU?

YAGU-RUMA...

NEXT TIME, LEAVE THE SHEATH TOO. THINK OF THE GUY WHO HAS TO HOLD IT FOR YOU.

HERE.

I'VE GOT NO USE FOR A FELLA WHO CAN'T RISK HIS LIFE FOR HIS FAMILY.

YOU'RE QUITE CLUMSY, AREN'T YOU?

I HEAR KEITH GANDOR IS FINE, BY THE WAY.

IF YOU'D MENTIONED PUTTING THE GANDORS IN OUR DEBT, YOU COULD HAVE MOBILIZED THE WHOLE MARTILLO FAMILY.

!? YOU MEAN IT, RONNY!?

I DON'T UNDERSTAND, BUT WE'RE GETTING THAT TREATED.

I DID NOT THINK OF THAT!!

...WELL, NEVER MIND.

I WONDER WHAT KIND OF GANGSTER YOU'LL BE.

OH...

OH......!
MY......
MY SAN
GENNARO
...!!

I GAVE
YOU THE
"LIQUOR"
BECAUSE
I THOUGHT
I COULD
USE YOU,
BUT...

WHAT A
DISGRACE.

ZA
(SHUFF)

PON
(PAT)

WE
TRANS-
PORTED
THE
LIQUOR ON
SCHEDULE.

WE MUST
NOT BEND
TO EVIL....!

KA
(TAK)

PLEASE
GRANT
ME YOUR
GUIDANCE!!
I MUST
NOT...THE
RIGHTEOUS
MUST
NOT...

KA
(TAK)

ズルル *ZURURU*

ズル *ZURU (SLURP)*

HUH?

I DON'T NEED YOU ANYMORE.

ばさ *BASA (FLAP)*

...HMPH. AS I THOUGHT— EATING INCOMPETENTS...

...ADDS NOTHING TO MY KNOWLEDGE.

TICK

TICK

TICK

TICK

TICK

TICK
TICK

I HAVEN'T HAD AN UGLY DREAM LIKE THAT......IN A VERY LONG TIME.

HEY, MAIZA!

MAIZA! GOOD MORNING.

WHY NOT TAKE TODAY OFF...?

FIRO, ARE YOUR INJURIES ALL RIGHT?

I'M FINE!

GOOD MORNING.

THAT'S WHY HE SHOULDN'T BE SO RECKLESS.

FIRO'S ALWAYS GETTING HIMSELF BUSTED UP.

PEOPLE...... DIE QUITE EASILY, YOU KNOW.

"TRUST YOUR FAMILY."

WELL YEAH, BUT...

I'M NOT THAT FRAGILE.

140

WELL, EVEN IF HE GOT AWAY, IT'S AMAZING THAT YOU FOUND HIM!

I MEAN, THAT WAS *THAT* GUY, RIGHT?

THE GUY WHO GAVE YOU THOSE... THAT PRIEST YOU CORNERED. IN THE END, HE DIDN'T DIE EITHER, RIGHT?

YEP. PEOPLE ARE TOUGHER THAN YOU'D THINK.

HA HA HA

HA!

THE "PHANTOM FATHER" FROM THE RUMORS!

WHAT WAS THE ACTUAL PHANTOM FATHER LIKE?

AND?

HE CAN DO STUFF WHEN HE TRIES!

WHEN I HEARD FIRO HAD HIGHTAILED IT OUTTA HERE, I FIGURED HE WOULDN'T BE ABLE TO DO NOTHIN' AND WOULD COME BACK EMPTY-HANDED!!

WASHA (RUFFLE) WASHA わしゃ わしゃ

141

...BUT I HEAR HE WAS INVOLVED.

I DUNNO WHAT HAPPENED AT THE CHURCH...

!?

THE CHURCH BURNED DOWN, BUT EVERYBODY'S FINE.

THERE WAS A FIRE SCARE AT AN ABANDONED CHURCH THAT DAY TOO. THAT HAVE ANYTHING TO DO WITH HIM!?

AND EVEN WHERE HE'D BLED...

HML

GASHI (GRAB)

I KNOW WE HURT HIM...

...BUT THE NEXT THING WE KNEW, HE'D BE FINE.

HE WAS AS WEIRD AS THE RUMORS SAY.

WHAT SORT OF MAN WAS HE?

NO...
I DON'T
THINK
SO......

FRIEND
OF
YOURS,
MAIZA?

LIGHT
BROWN,
KINDA
SHORT
HAIR...
MAYBE
IN HIS
TWENTIES
...?

HE WAS
TALLISH,
AND HE
LOOKED
PRETTY
SKINNY.

WHAT,
THEN?
ARE YOU
SAYING
THERE'S A
GUY WHO
REALLY
DOESN'T
DIE?

IT
DIDN'T FEEL
LIKE AN
ILLUSION
......

RATS!

IF HE
WAS YOUR
FRIEND,
I COULDA
ASKED HIM
HOW THE
TRICK IS
DONE.

OR
WAS HE A
HOMUNCULUS
SOME
ALCHEMIST
MADE?

DID
SOME DEAD
GUY GO
VAMPIRE?

NOW
THAT'S A
TRICK I'D
LOVE TO
LEARN.

IMMORTALITY THOUGH! I COULD DO STUFF WITH THAT.

YOU'RE THE ONE WHO SAID IT WASN'T FAKE.

ARE YOU MAKING FUN OF ME, RANDY?

IF YOU KEEP LIVING, YOU ONLY ACCUMULATE REGRETS.

NEVER MIND THAT. I HAVE A LITTLE BUSINESS AT THE CHURCH YOU MENTIONED...

WELL, NO, BUT...

OH. SURE, I'LL TAKE YOU OVER THERE.

SIMPLY NOT DYING WOULDN'T MAKE YOU OMNIPOTENT, WOULD IT?

144

IF YOU WOULD THEN, FIRO.

ちら
CHIRA
(GLANCE)

YOU SHOULD BE ABLE TO SEE IT SOON.

IT STILL LOOKS ABOUT THE SAME ON THE OUTSIDE.

IS IT ALL IN MY HEAD?

MAIZA SEEMS KINDA TENSE.

WAIT! CAN I HELP YOU WITH ANYTHING!?

UH...

THANK YOU FOR COMING THIS FAR WITH ME.

HUH?

I SEE. IN THAT CASE, YOU DON'T HAVE TO TAKE ME ANY FARTHER.

IF YOU'RE SEARCHING THE CHURCH, MORE PEOPLE WOULD BE......

FIRO.

IT'S NOTHING TO DO WITH YOU.

...I SEE.

......

I TOOK THESE LICKS FOR THE BROTHERS I GREW UP WITH...

...BUT I'M PREPARED TO TAKE A BEATING FOR MY MARTILLO "FAMILY" TOO.

THEN I'LL BE...

MAIZA.

SO IF IT EVER LOOKS LIKE THERE'S SOMETHING I CAN DO, TELL ME.

......

I'M SAYING YOU GROW FASTER WITH EACH INJURY.

SO YOU'RE CALLING ME SIMPLE? IS THAT IT?

むす
MUSU
(SULK)

...WHY YOU'RE ALWAYS GETTING HURT.

HUH!?

YOU... CONFRONT EVERYTHING STRAIGHT ON. I WONDER IF THAT'S ...

...THOUGHT I SHOULD CONFRONT MATTERS HEAD-ON AS WELL.

......I ONLY ...

SOMETHING BAD HAPPENED, LONG AGO.

I'D BEEN THINKING ABOUT IT.

YEAH, LEAVE IT TO ME!

I'M SORRY TO HAVE WORRIED YOU.

IF THERE'S A CRISIS, I'LL BE COUNTING ON YOU.

KA (TAK)

...... "IF THERE'S A CRISIS"...

SHOULD I LOOK FOR HIM ON MY OWN?

SHOULD I AVOID GOING OUT?

I MUSTN'T PULL THE MARTILLOS INTO THIS.

I WONDER WHICH WOULD CAUSE LESS TROUBLE FOR THE ORGANIZATION ......

...IF I LEFT THEM.

I SUPPOSE IT WOULD BE BEST ...

BUT "LEAVING" WASN'T THE FIRST CHOICE THAT CAME TO MIND, WHICH MEANS...

THIS MUST BE IT.

...I'VE CHANGED AS WELL...

GASA (RUSTLE)

THE PHANTOM FATHER PROBABLY ISN'T ONE OF THE OLD GROUP......THE MEMBERS FROM THE SHIP.

STILL, IT NEVER HURTS TO BE CAREFUL.

KA (TAK)

I SEE I'M NOT THE FIRST ONE HERE.

WELL, WELL...

BIKU (FLINCH)

JUST LIKE YOU...

...LITTLE THIEF.

IN MY POSITION, I PREFER NOT TO DEAL WITH THE POLICE, TO BE HONEST.

JIRI (SIDLE)

WHAT'RE YOU......? A COP...!?

HE GETS DRUNK, BUSTS STUFF UP, FEELS BAD, THEN DRINKS AGAIN TO FORGET IT.

MY DAD'S AT A SPEAKEASY AGAIN TODAY......!

WHOSE FAULT DO YOU THINK IT IS I'M SCAVENGING HERE!!?

SHUT UP...!

THAT'S WHY WE'VE GOT PROHIBITION...

LIQUOR'S BAD, RIGHT?

BOTH NOW AND LONG AGO ......

ZU CCLUNK

THE FOOLS... ARE THE HUMANS WHO GIVE IN TO THE TEMPTATION OF LIQUOR.

DOGAGA
(WHUD)

!?

STILL...

UGH
...

152

zu
(SHLP)
zu

AH...
AH...

!!
GOPO
(BLORP)

I GAVE IN TO THE TEMPTATION OF LIQUOR TOO, IN A WAY......

...WELL...

zu
zu
zu

I'LL GIVE YOU THE KNOWLEDGE YOU SEEK.

YOU, THE ALCHEMIST WHO SUMMONED ME...

...EVERYTHING ABOUT "IMMORTALITY."

...AND LIVE IT YOURSELVES.

IMPRESSIONS VARY WIDELY, YOU SEE.

THE ANSWER IS TO DRINK THAT LIQUOR...

WHY...?

YOU DON'T... DIE?

...THAT'S NOT QUITE TRUE.

STRICTLY SPEAKING ...

AND... PLEASE REFRAIN FROM TELLING ANYONE YOU MET ME HERE.

IT LOOKS AS THOUGH YOUR THINGS SURVIVED. THAT'S GOOD.

ドサ
DOSA
(WHUMP)

だーっ
DAAA
(DASH)

SO FAST...

コク
KOKU
(NOD)

コク
KOKU

...BUT I DO HAVE TO FACE IT...

IT MAY BE THE RESULT OF WHAT I WISHED FOR...

パキ
PAKI
(SNAP)

I DIDN'T MEAN TO FRIGHTEN HIM, BUT I SUPPOSE...

...THAT'S THE NORMAL REACTION.

IT'S ALREADY BEEN, WHAT...... *TWO HUNDRED YEARS?*

SOMEDAY, I WILL SETTLE THINGS WITH "HIM," WITHOUT FAIL.

SINCE NEITHER OF US IS LIMITED BY OUR LIFE SPAN...

NO, WE HAVEN'T FOUND HIM YET!

WAS HE THERE?

...AND END UP FEARING DEATH RIGHT OFF THE BAT...

TO THINK WE'D GAIN IMMORTAL-ITY...

HE'S ALREADY *EATEN* SEVERAL OF OUR COMPANIONS. IT'S DANGEROUS TO LET OUR GUARD DOWN.

IT'LL JUST GROW BACK ANYWAY.

JUST FOR THE RECORD, IT'S ALL RIGHT IF WE TAKE OFF HIS HEAD, ISN'T IT?

GHAH ...

ZURU
(SHLOO)

ズル

BASA
(SHUF)

WHAT HAVE YOU DONE...

...SZILARD ...?

—AND SO EVERYTHING TWINES TOGETHER. THE WHEEL OF FORTUNE TUMBLES DOWN THE SPIRAL.

SO...

IT'S JUST BURSTING WITH IT!

THIS IS OUR CITY OF HOPE, IS IT!?

BACCANO! 1930
[THE ROLLING BOOTLEGS]
TO BE CONTINUED......

WHAT'S WITH THOSE GUYS ...?

NIKA (GRIN)

BACCANO! 1 **END**

NEXT
[BACCANO!] 2
1930 NY
KEEP ON ROLLIN'!!

Cut, with great reluctance, due to page limitations...

DIALOGUE WRITTEN BY NARITA-SENSEI, JUST FOR THIS MANGA

SILENT MOVIES, HUH!?

APPARENTLY HE'S TAKEN A SHINE TO A CERTAIN LADY PIANIST.

[From Chapter 2, Page 62, Panel 3]

KEITH PREFERS SILENT MOVIES TO FESTIVALS.

THEY SAY IT OPENS NEXT MONTH.

FROM WHAT I HEAR, THE JAZZ SINGER MOVIE THEY'RE MAKING NOW IS AMAZING.

I BET THE TALKIES ARE GONNA GIVE 'EM A RUN FOR THEIR MONEY.

YOUR PIANIST MIGHT BE OUT OF A JOB SOON, HUH?

IF THAT HAPPENS, YOU CAN JUST TAKE CARE OF HER YOURSELF!

HEY, KEITH, DON'T LOOK LIKE THAT!

End

SPECIAL THANKS

☆ ORIGINAL WORK
Ryohgo Narita

☆ CHARACTER DESIGN
Katsumi Enami

☆ SUPERVISING EDITORS
(Dengeki Bunko)
Atsushi Wada
(Young GanGan)
Kazuhide Shimizu

☆ STAFF
Yoshichika Eguchi
Noriyuki Yuno
Yuuto Saito
Nora

☆ BOOK DESIGN
Yoko Iwasa

And you!

BACCANO! TIMES
CAROL'S NOTES

UNIDENTIFIED FLYING CREATURE...!?

While Little Italy celebrated during the San Gennaro Festival, a figure was spotted leaping over the rooftops!! Was it a reckless human or some other life-form...? New York is a mysterious place.

Vol.
1

BACCANO!

Original works *Ryohgo Narita*

Art works
Shinta Fujimoto

Character design
Katsumi Enami

Since
1927

BACCANO! ①

S0-ADP-652

Shinta Fujimoto
Ryohgo Narita
Katsumi Enami

Translation: Taylor Engel • **Lettering: Rochelle Gancio**

BACCANO! vol.1
© 2016 Ryohgo Narita
© 2016 Shinta Fujimoto / SQUARE ENIX CO., LTD.
Licensed by KADOKAWA CORPORATION ASCII MEDIA WORKS
First published in Japan in 2016 by SQUARE ENIX CO., LTD. English translation rights arranged with SQUARE ENIX CO., LTD. and Yen Press, LLC through Tuttle-Mori Agency, Inc.

English translation © 2018 by SQUARE ENIX CO., LTD.

Yen Press
1290 Avenue of the Americas
New York, NY 10104

Visit us at yenpress.com
facebook.com/yenpress
twitter.com/yenpress
yenpress.tumblr.com
instagram.com/yenpress

First Yen Press Edition: January 2018
The chapters in this volume were originally published as ebooks by Yen Press.

Yen Press is an imprint of Yen Press, LLC.
The Yen Press name and logo are trademarks of Yen Press, LLC.

The publisher is not responsible for websites (or their content) that are not owned by the publisher.

Library of Congress Control Number: 2016910571

ISBNs: 978-0-316-55278-3 (paperback)
       978-0-316-48002-4 (ebook)

10 9 8 7 6 5 4 3 2 1

BVG

Printed in the United States of America